S0-BCM-569

The KidHaven Science Library

The Mars Rovers

by Lucile Davis

KIDHAVEN PRESS

An imprint of Thomson Gale, a part of The Thomson Corporation

THOMSON

GALE

Detroit • New York • San Francisco • San Diego • New Haven, Conn.
Waterville, Maine • London • Munich

© 2005 Thomson Gale, a part of The Thomson Corporation.

Thomson and Star Logo are trademarks and Gale and KidHaven Press are registered trademarks used herein under license.

For more information, contact
KidHaven Press
27500 Drake Rd.
Farmington Hills, MI 48331-3535
Or you can visit our Internet site at http://www.gale.com

LIBRARY OF CONGRESS CATALOGING-IN-PUBLICATION DATA

Davis, Lucile, 1944–
    The Mars Rovers / by Lucile Davis.
        p. cm. — (The KidHaven science library)
    Summary: Discusses the Mars rovers, how they work, and what they are researching.
    Includes bibliographical references and index.
    ISBN 0-7377-3074-9 (hard cover : alk. paper)
    1. Mars (Planet)—Exploration—Juvenile literature. 2. Roving vehicles (Astronautics)—Juvenile literature. I. Title. II. Series.
    QB641.D38 2004
523.43—dc22
<div align="right">2004008235</div>

Printed in the United States of America

Contents

Chapter 1

Mission to Mars

Has there ever been life on Mars? The United States sent two robotic **geologists** to the red planet to find out. The Mars Exploration Rover (MER) robots were built to withstand the extreme conditions on the surface of Mars. Each robot had its own spot on Mars to explore. The Mars rover named *Spirit* landed in a crater. On the other side of the planet, the rover named *Opportunity* bounced down on a wide plain.

The robots were to study rocks and soil layers on Mars for signs of water. Scientists have learned that life begins in water. The sediments deposited by water in soil and rocks hold the answer to the question about life on Mars.

Why We Explore

Humans want to know if life on Earth is an accident of nature or a regular part of an orderly universe. Interest in what lies beyond this planet started when humans began to explore the lights in the nighttime sky. People in ancient times thought the lights were gods. The Greeks discovered that some of the lights in the night sky moved. One of these moving lights glowed red. The Greeks believed it to be Ares, the god of war. The Romans also believed the red light in the sky was the god of war. They called him Mars.

Mars is named after the Roman god of war, pictured in this ancient sculpture.

People continued to watch and study the lights in the sky. The moving lights became known as planets. The others were called stars. The invention of the telescope in 1608 helped people see Mars and the other planets as more than just lights in the sky. In the 1870s, Italian astronomer Giovanni Schiaparelli reported seeing *canali,* or channels, on Mars. A misunderstanding of the translation of the word *canali* led some people to think Schiaparelli had seen canals on Mars. Canals are artificially created bodies of water. This made many people believe the Mars canals were built by beings who lived on the planet.

Myth and Reality

The idea of life on Mars sparked people's imaginations. Writers began creating tales of Martian life and civilization. Through books, songs, radio programs, and movies Martians were shown as intelligent and able to travel in space. Some writers imagined the Martians might even invade Earth. H.G. Wells wrote of this possible invasion in his 1898 novel, *The War of the Worlds.* Early in the 1900s Edgar Rice Burroughs, best known for his *Tarzan* stories, created adventure tales of life on Mars. Burroughs renamed Mars. He called the planet Barsoom.

Scientists wanted to do more than imagine life on Mars. They wanted to know for sure if it ever

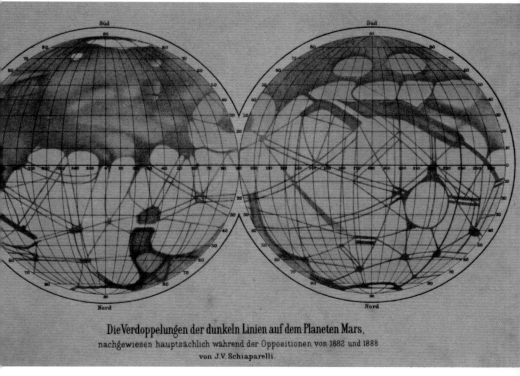

Die Verdoppelungen der dunkeln Linien auf dem Planeten Mars,
nachgewiesen hauptsächlich während der Oppositionen von 1882 und 1888
von J.V. Schiaparelli.

*In 1877 Italian astronomer Giovanni Schiaparelli drew
this detailed map of Mars showing channels on its surface.*

existed. By the middle of the twentieth century, scientists were ready to have a closer look at the planet. Thirty-three missions to Mars have been launched by three nations—Japan, Russia (formerly the Union of Soviet Socialist Republics), and the United States. The European Space Agency, operated by the nations of the European Union, joined the Mars exploration effort in June 2003. As of summer 2004, the U.S. Mars missions have been the most successful.

U.S. Missions to Mars

The U.S. National Aeronautics and Space Administration (NASA) created the Mariner program to take a closer look at Mars. Mariner was a photographic mission. On November 5, 1964, NASA sent *Mariner 3* toward Mars. Equipment failure ended that mission. Twenty-three days later, *Mariner 4* succeeded and sent seventy-five photographs back to Earth for scientists to study. The last one, *Mariner 9*, took off in May 1971 and sent back over seven thousand pictures of the Martian surface.

The photographs taken by *Mariner 4* allowed NASA scientists to choose the best locations on the planet for closer study. The Viking program sent orbiting **modules** and landing vehicles to Mars. The Viking mission conducted chemistry experiments and took more detailed photographs of the planet. Two orbiters and two landers explored Mars between 1976 and 1987. The landers returned over fifty thousand images of the planet. They also provided NASA scientists with information about the planet's atmosphere and weather.

What Scientists Learned About Mars

Neither the Mariner nor the Viking missions to Mars found any signs of life on the planet. What they did find was a cold world of wild storms and an atmosphere of carbon dioxide gas. The surface temperature averages minus 64 degrees Fahrenheit (minus 53 degrees Celsius). Winds blow up to eighty miles an hour (forty meters per second), sometimes causing whirlwinds known as dust

In 1976 Viking 1 *took this and thousands of other photographs of the red, rocky surface of Mars.*

devils. The atmosphere is 95 percent carbon dioxide gas, 2.7 percent nitrogen, and 1.6 percent argon. Humans breathe in oxygen and expel carbon dioxide. Since there is no oxygen in the Mars atmosphere, humans could not survive there.

Scientists knew human exploration of Mars was not possible, but the Viking landers proved machines could do the job. NASA launched the *Mars Global Surveyor* to the planet in 1996. This

NASA engineers prepare the Mars Pathfinder *and its rover (pictured between its solar panels) for launch in 1996.*

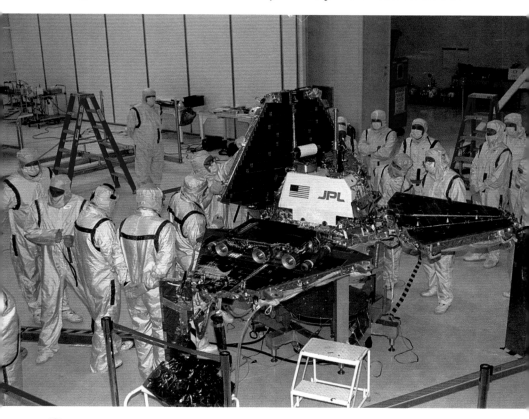

orbiter's mission was to provide scientists with a high-detail map of Mars.

The detailed maps from *Surveyor* helped scientists pick the best locations for more on-planet exploration. *Mars Pathfinder* explored the planet for three months in 1997. Four years later another orbiter helped scientists study the planet's environment. Launched in 2001, *Mars Odyssey*'s mission was to study ground composition and take **thermal** images of the planet. Thermal images show temperature levels of an area or mass. *Odyssey*'s study revealed some interesting information about what scientists referred to as the Mars "polar ice caps."

A Hint of Water

Information from the *Mars Odyssey* mission show the ice caps to be ice crystals in the soil. The frosted soil gives the appearance of ice caps like those on Earth. The polar ice caps of Earth, however, are solid ice. If the Mars ice caps indicate there is water below the surface of the planet, then it is possible there may have been life on the planet. But water must be in a liquid form to aid in the creation of life.

There are signs water might have been there during the planet's early history. Mars is not a dead planet. It has a **molten** core. Pressure from the molten core builds and explodes onto the surface.

In 2002 NASA's Hubble Telescope took this photograph, which clearly shows the polar ice caps of Mars.

Pictures of a 9,000-foot (2.74-km) volcano taken by *Mariner 9* reveal this information. Where heat meets ice, water forms and life could develop. Did volcanic activity on Mars melt water crystals in the soil on the planet's surface? Was there water on the surface of the planet long enough to allow organisms to develop? These are the questions scientists seek to answer with the ongoing missions to Mars.

Chapter 2

Leaving Earth Behind

The Mars Exploration Rover program continues the search for signs of water and the possibility that life once existed on Mars. The Mars Exploration Rover mission began June 10, 2003. On that day a Delta II rocket headed for Mars with the rover named *Spirit* tucked in its nose capsule. But *Spirit* and its twin rover, *Opportunity*, did not get a direct flight from Earth to Mars. Their delivery to Mars was planned in several stages.

The hardest part of the journey to Mars was getting away from the gravitational pull of Earth. A three-stage launch vehicle was required to lift the rover spacecraft off the launchpad and away from Earth's atmosphere. The three stages were the launch rocket, a smaller rocket below the nose cone, and a high-powered motor located just under the rover spacecraft. A lot of rocket power and fuel were required. On the pad the launch vehicle weighed 628,820 pounds (285,228 kilograms). The spacecraft containing the rover only weighed 2,355 pounds (1,070 kilograms). The three-stage rocket and most of the weight would be gone by the time the spacecraft left Earth's orbit.

Spirit Goes First

Spirit drew the express route to Mars. Every twenty-six months Earth, Mars, and the Sun line up to create the easiest and most energy efficient path between Earth and Mars. This alignment happened in June 2003. After *Spirit* was on its way, it

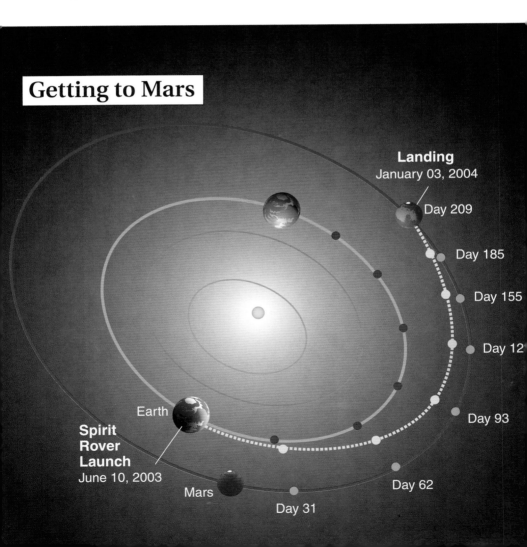

Getting to Mars

Landing
January 03, 2004

Day 209

Day 185

Day 155

Day 12

Day 93

Earth

Spirit Rover Launch
June 10, 2003

Mars

Day 31

Day 62

took a month to clear the launch site at Cape Canaveral Air Station in Florida and set up the next launch vehicle. By then Mars had moved away from Earth, so *Opportunity* had a longer trip. It therefore required more fuel and a rocket able to lift the heavier load. Each rover was sent toward Mars on a Delta II launch vehicle.

Spirit began its journey to Mars on June 10, 2003, at 1:58:47 P.M. eastern daylight time. The three-stage Delta II 7925 rocket looked like a fat pencil standing on its eraser with nine crayons tied around it. The main launch rocket needed nine smaller rockets to help lift the heavy vehicle off the pad. When the flight director yelled "launch," the main rocket and six of the nine smaller rockets fired. The base of the rocket disappeared in billows of smoke as the heavy vehicle lifted off the pad. Moments later the last three small rockets fired. That ended the first stage of *Spirit*'s journey away from Earth.

Wrapped in a Nose Cone

The main rocket and nine smaller rockets separated from the nose cone. This left a much smaller and lighter vehicle to continue toward Earth's outer atmosphere. The nose cone contained stages two and three of the launch vehicle, plus the spacecraft. Called the payload **fairing**, the nose cone is a protective cover for the launch vehicle and spacecraft. Its tapered, round nose helped cut down on the wind resistance as the vehicle moved toward Earth's outer atmosphere. At 80 miles (130 km) above Earth, the fairing or nose cone was **jettisoned**.

Spirit and its spacecraft soared toward Earth's outer atmosphere powered by the second stage of Delta II. The second stage fired twice. The first firing sent the launch vehicle into a low Earth orbit. The second firing positioned the vehicle to depart for Mars. When this positioning was complete, the second stage separated from the Delta II launch vehicle.

On the Way to Mars

The third stage of Delta II gave the MER spacecraft the boost needed to pick up speed to escape Earth's gravitational pull. The third stage launched the spacecraft toward Mars. The Delta II launch vehicle fell back toward Earth and burned up in the outer atmosphere. Once the spacecraft was on its way to Mars, NASA's spaceflight engineers at Cape Canaveral alerted the scientists at the Jet Propulsion Laboratory in Pasadena, California. NASA scientists there would control and monitor the rest of *Spirit*'s trip to and mission on Mars.

Spirit's journey between Earth and Mars took seven months. NASA scientists used the time to

With a cloud of smoke, the Delta II rocket lifts off from Florida's Kennedy Space Center on June 10, 2003.

Leaving Earth Behind

make corrections in the flight path. They also test-ed instruments and monitored the activity inside the spacecraft.

Mars Just Ahead

Just a few days into January 2004 computers on board the spacecraft signaled that Mars lay just ahead. Rockets on board the craft fired to rotate the vehicle into position for **descent**. Fifteen minutes before the spacecraft entered the Martian atmosphere, the craft's heat shield jettisoned. The spacecraft entered the Mars atmosphere traveling 12,000 miles per hour (5,400 m per second). The friction of traveling through the atmosphere helped slow the spacecraft to about 960 miles per hour (430 m per second). Five miles (about 8 km) from the surface of the planet a parachute opened to help slow the descent. Thirty seconds later a long strap, still attached to the parachute, lowered *Spirit*'s lander to within about 1.5 miles (2.4 km) of the planet's surface, then dropped it.

Gas generators on *Spirit*'s lander blew up air bags around the vehicle. *Spirit*'s lander now resembled a pyramid of tan bowling balls. The air bags cushioned the landing. The air-bag-wrapped lander bounced a number of times before coming to rest right side up.

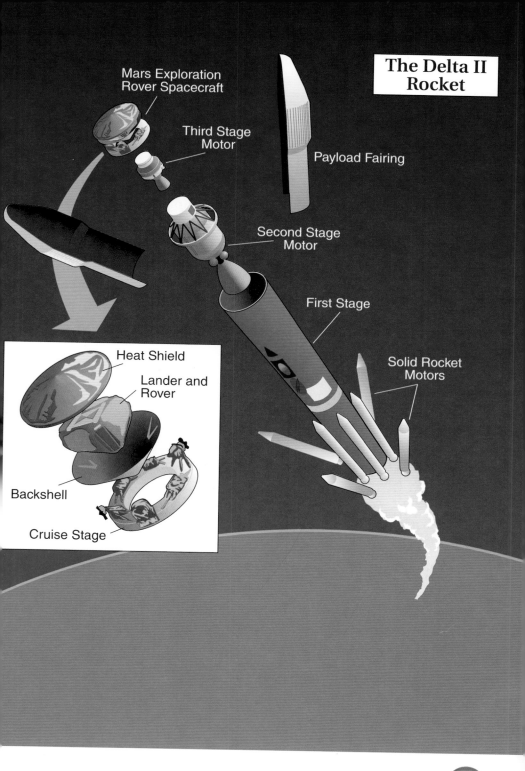

The Delta II Rocket

Mars Exploration Rover Spacecraft

Third Stage Motor

Payload Fairing

Second Stage Motor

First Stage

Solid Rocket Motors

Heat Shield

Lander and Rover

Backshell

Cruise Stage

*Inflated seconds before landing, giant air bags protected
Spirit's lander as it touched down on the Martian surface.*

Rover Revealed

The lander air bags began to deflate twelve minutes after settling in an upright position on Mars.
The process took about an hour. Then four solar
panels around the lander opened. This operation
took about twenty minutes. Had the vehicle landed on its side the panel opening would have taken
about thirty-five minutes. An upside-down land-

ing could have required over an hour to right the lander and open the solar panels.

The opened lander panels revealed *Spirit*. The rover's first official move was to unfold its solar **array** panels. Next *Spirit* took pictures of its surroundings. This helped the rover identify any problems it might face once it left its lander.

The rover depended on sunlight to power its computer and equipment. This meant *Spirit* had

This photograph taken by Spirit's *rover shows the lander with its deflated air bags and open solar panels.*

to work during the Martian day that lasts twenty-four hours, thirty-nine minutes, and thirty-five seconds. *Spirit* landed four hours before the Martian sunset. It took pictures and sent them back to NASA scientists on Earth, then shut down for the night. At dawn *Spirit* began surveying the Martian landscape.

A month later the rover *Opportunity* followed *Spirit* to Mars. By February 2004 both rovers were busy studying Mars and sending their findings back to Earth. The rover robots were designed to operate much like a living being. And like living beings, the rovers experienced some trouble.

Chapter 3

How the Rovers Worked

*S**pirit**,* like its twin rover, *Opportunity,* was about the size of a golf cart. In a sense, the rover's parts were like those that any living creature needed to stay alive. Its body protected vital parts and its computer brain processed information. Sensing devices, such as cameras mounted on a neck, allowed pictures to be taken from human eye level. A robotic arm could reach out to touch and test the planet's surface. Six wheels, instead of two legs, gave the rover stability and the ability to move.

Batteries and solar panels provided energy. Communications were sent and received through antennas. The Mars Exploration Rover was designed to do the work of a field geologist while on Mars. Like a human geologist, the rover took pictures and samples of Martian rocks and soil. The humanlike parts of the rover allowed it to perform these tasks.

The rover's body protected its vital organs. The body, called the warm electronics box or WEB,

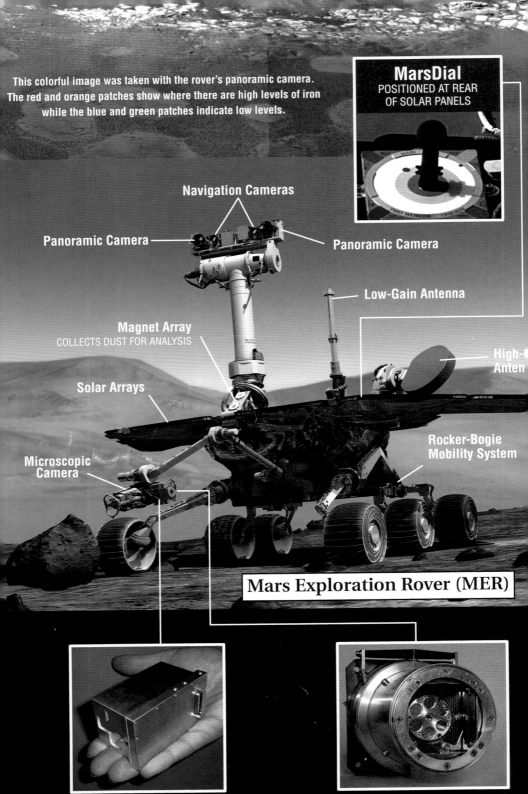

This colorful image was taken with the rover's panoramic camera. The red and orange patches show where there are high levels of iron while the blue and green patches indicate low levels.

MarsDial
POSITIONED AT REAR OF SOLAR PANELS

Navigation Cameras

Panoramic Camera

Panoramic Camera

Low-Gain Antenna

Magnet Array
COLLECTS DUST FOR ANALYSIS

High-Gain Antenna

Solar Arrays

Rocker-Bogie Mobility System

Microscopic Camera

Mars Exploration Rover (MER)

Moessbauer Spectrometer

Alpha Particle X-ray Spectrometer

contained the computer and batteries. NASA engineers considered them the rover's brains and heart. Gold paint insulated the computer and batteries from the night temperatures on Mars. Temperatures can drop to minus 140 degrees Fahrenheit (minus 96 degrees Celsius).

The robot body housed powerful computer equipment that could endure the high levels of radiation from the sun. The computer also monitored the robot's health to make sure temperature levels were fine and the robot's programming continued to function normally.

Batteries powered by solar panels were the power plant or heart of each robot. Just like the human heart, the batteries kept everything on the robot working. The batteries powered the computer and electronics that ran the robot's head, neck, arm, and wheels.

Head and Neck

Equipment that extended out from the body of the rover helped it investigate Mars. This equipment included cameras, a robotic arm, and wheels to help move the rover around.

The rover had nine cameras. The two cameras mounted on the extendable neck helped with navigation. These cameras were called Navcams. Another pair of cameras on the rover's head were Pancams. These two cameras were used for science investigation. They gave the rover a **panoramic** view of Mars—in color. Four cameras mounted on the front and back of the body were "hazard avoidance cameras" or Hazcams. The cameras had a wide field of vision, about 120 degrees, to help the rover avoid running into anything. A science camera mounted on the robotic arm allowed the rover to take close-up pictures of rocks and soil.

Arm and Legs

The rover's robotic arm made it possible for scientists to reach out to investigate the Martian surface. Three joints gave humanlike flexibility to the arm. A clamp at the end of the arm acted as a hand. There were four tools at the end of the arm. These scientific tools included a microscope, a **spectrometer**, an X-ray spectrometer, and a RAT (rock **abrasion** tool). The microscope provided a very close view of rocks and soil. The spectrome-

Special cameras on Spirit's *head took this photograph, the first*

ters analyzed the elements of the soil. They looked for simple chemical elements such as iron and sulfur. Analyzing elements of rocks and soil were part of the robot's experiments to determine if bodies of water once existed on Mars.

Six wheels moved the rover from place to place. Each wheel had its own individual motor. This allowed any wheel to move independent of the others. The two front and two back wheels also had independent steering motors. This made it possible for the rover to turn a full 360 degrees. The rover could climb at a tilt of 45 degrees. Its tires had cleats that gripped the planet surface to help the vehicle move and climb.

Communication

The rover's communication center was in its computer. All commands to move and do research came from the NASA scientists on Earth. What the

...noramic image of the Martian surface.

Spirit photographed this group of rocks (left) before taking a detailed close-up of one rock (right). Spirit *then brushed the dus*

rover learned was not kept in its computer. Instead, the computer sent the information back to NASA's computers at the Jet Propulsion Laboratory. If the NASA scientists could not communicate with the robot, its mission was over. *Spirit's* mission nearly ended just as it was getting started.

Spirit Rover on Mars

Two days after *Spirit* landed on Mars, NASA scientists found the rover had a problem. Routine tests showed *Spirit's* electrical system did not work the way it should. The problem seemed minor, but the NASA scientists knew it had to be fixed before the rover could move off its lander. The original

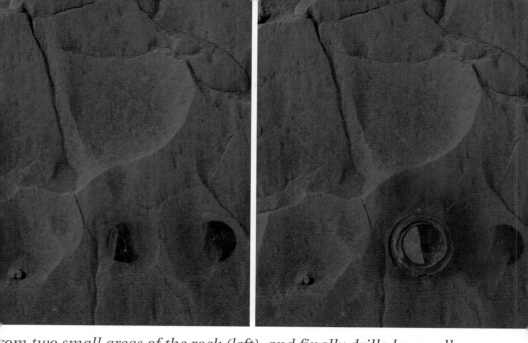

...om two small areas of the rock (left), and finally drilled a small ...ole (right).

plan was to move the rover off the lander one week after landing. Scientists continued to work toward that goal.

Spirit's ability to take and send pictures was not affected by the electrical problem. The first pictures from Spirit showed a landscape of sharp and smooth rocks. Spirit transmitted more pictures to Earth as scientists continued to test the rover's readiness to roll off the lander.

Rolling with Rover

About ten days after landing on Mars, Spirit moved on to the planet's surface. Spirit's electrical problem seemed to be fixed. NASA scientists were

The instruments at the end of Spirit's *robotic arm clean the surface of a rock before collecting a sample.*

eager to see what *Spirit* would find on the surface. Instructions from NASA extended the robot's arm to examine the fine-grained Martian soil. Five days of more pictures and more soil sampling followed. On the morning of January 19, 2004, scientists commanded *Spirit* to go to a rock called

"Adirondack." *Spirit* rolled to the rock and extended its arm. The robotic arm took a spectrometer reading of the soil around the rock.

Spirit's next duty was to grind the surface of Adirondack in order to see what lay inside the rock. The robotic arm extended toward the rock, then stopped. The rover quit responding. Three days later NASA ground controllers managed to get a response from the rover. The only thing *Spirit* said was, "I'm OK." The rover could monitor its own health and report. It could not do anything else.

Fixing the Rover

Scientists discovered *Spirit's* problem was in its software. The software had to be deleted and then reloaded. *Spirit* came back to life just before its twin rover, *Opportunity*, landed on the other side of Mars. January 25, 2004, turned out to be a great day for the scientists at NASA. By the end of the day they knew there were two functioning rover robots on Mars. The search for water on the planet would get under way at dawn the following day.

Chapter 4

The Robots' Research

The rovers' search for water had been planned in advance of their flights to Mars. More than one hundred scientists had spent two years looking at 155 possible sites for the rovers' landings. The locations had to be safe and be likely places to find signs of water.

Scientists decided on two landing sites located around the planet's equator. *Spirit* rover would land in Gusev Crater. This site appeared to have had a lake in it a long time ago. *Opportunity* would bounce down on Meridiani Planum, a smooth plain rich in gray hematite. This gray mineral is a type of iron oxide usually, but not always, formed in connection with water.

Spirit in Gusev Crater

Gusev Crater is about the size of the state of Connecticut. An asteroid or comet impact dug the crater perhaps as many as 4 billion years ago. One of the planet's largest valleys has a branch that extends into Gusev Crater. It is possible the large valley could have been carved out by running water more than 2 billion years ago. Water flowing down the valley would have pooled in Gusev Crater. The crater was thought to be relatively flat and held great promise for signs of water. This made it a perfect site for a rover landing.

pirit Rover Landing Site: Columbia Memorial Station

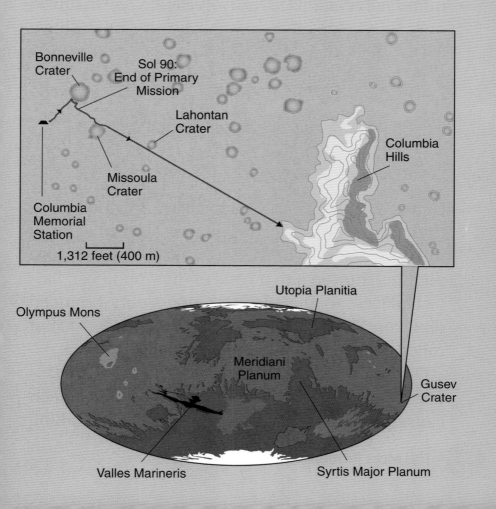

Once *Spirit's* software was fixed, it continued its search for signs of water. The rover completed several geological experiments on the rock, Adirondack. *Spirit* discovered the rock was volcanic basalt. The rover moved on to a spot in the crater that showed signs the soil had expanded and contracted. The same soil patterns on Earth appear in areas that are contracted and expanded by freezing and thawing when water is present in the soil. *Spirit* dug a hole in the Martian surface. It found bright material in the rock that looked like minerals crystallized out of water. *Spirit* found only small clues that a body of water might have existed in Gusev Crater. The rover *Opportunity* found much more evidence of water on its landing site, Meridiani Planum.

Opportunity to Meridiani

The Meridiani Planum is a bit larger than Gusev Crater. The place-name indicates its location close to the planet's prime meridian or equator. *Planum* means "plains." The name fits the area because pictures showed it to be one of the smoothest, flattest places on the planet. *Opportunity* bounced down on Meridiani Planum on January 25, 2004. It rolled off its lander a week later.

Opportunity's first pictures of Mars showed layers in the rocks. The layers could have been caused by running water, blowing wind, or falling

Opportunity *discov-
ered small round
rocks (microscopic
close-up, inset) in
the soil of the
Meridiani Planum.*

volcanic ash. The pictures also revealed large amounts of hematite in the soil. Several days later *Opportunity* used its microscope and spectrometer to take a closer look at the soil.

The tests on the soil verified the presence of hematite. Olivine, a common ingredient in volcanic rock, was also found. The tests also revealed a mystery. Small round rocks were discovered in the soil. The round rocks or spheres were gray and no larger than BBs. NASA scientists dubbed them "blueberries."

A Blueberry Mystery

Opportunity found blueberries all over its landing site. The little spheres were embedded in the rocks. Pictures of the rock-embedded blueberries showed the spheres were being released from the rocks by wind erosion. Due to the wind erosion process, blueberries were scattered all over the ground. *Opportunity* used its rock abrasion tool to study a rock at the site. It found more blueberries. After the rover dug a hole, it found blueberries deep in the Martian soil.

NASA scientists were puzzled. What were the blueberries made of and how did they get there? The BB-size spheres were too small for the spectrometer to discover what they contained. After a month of investigation *Opportunity* found a small crater in a large boulder. It was full of blueberries. The cluster of small spheres made a mass big enough for the spectrometer to take a reading. The blueberries were iron-bearing hematite. The crystallized mineral composition of the berries told scientists the little spheres were probably formed in a wet **environment**.

Opportunity found the hematite-filled blueberries just about every place it explored on Meridiani

Planum. The abundance of blueberries seemed to indicate the area *Opportunity* explored might have held a lot of water. Further investigation was needed, though. A rock outcropping could tell scientists whether the rocks were formed or altered by moving water. Rock formations that appear above

Opportunity Rover Landing Site: Eagle Crater

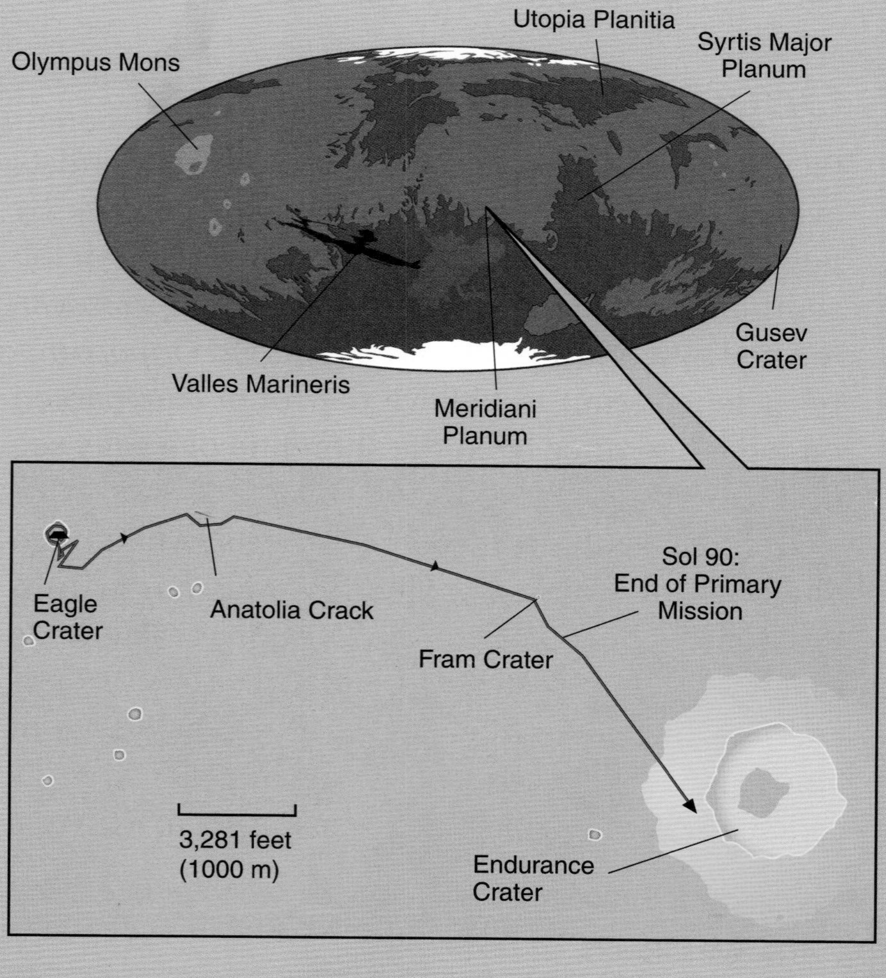

Olympus Mons

Utopia Planitia

Syrtis Major Planum

Gusev Crater

Valles Marineris

Meridiani Planum

Eagle Crater

Anatolia Crack

Fram Crater

Sol 90: End of Primary Mission

3,281 feet (1000 m)

Endurance Crater

ground show **strata**, or layers of soil and minerals. The layers are made when soil and minerals are deposited on the ground either by blowing wind, flowing lava, or running water.

The very first pictures *Opportunity* had taken of its surroundings showed a rock outcropping in the distance. With the discovery of the iron-bearing blueberries, scientists could not wait to have *Opportunity* examine it more closely. They sent the robot geologist toward the rock formation, which they had named "Upper Dells."

Opportunity by the Sea

Pictures from *Opportunity* showed NASA scientists evidence of **sediments** laid down in the rock by flowing water. Rock sample testing showed the sediments contained minerals found in rocks formed by a body of salt water. This led *Opportunity*'s science team to believe the robot was parked on what had once been the shoreline of a salty sea on Mars.

The rock sediments indicated the sea had been shallow, its waters rippled by Martian winds. Excitement swept through NASA as scientists absorbed the news. *Spirit* added to their excitement with information it had found evidence of underground water in Gusev Crater. These finds led scientists to plan an extension to the rovers' mission.

Mission Extended

The Mars Exploration Rover mission had original-
ly been set at ninety days. NASA scientists set this
timetable based on what they had learned from
the *Mars Pathfinder* mission in the late 1990s. The
Pathfinder rover had been expected to last only
seven days on Mars due to the harsh environment. It functioned for ninety days before the
planet's heat and weather ended the mission.

Using what they had learned from *Pathfinder*,
NASA scientists designed *Spirit* and *Opportunity*

*These rocks, with ripple patterns and sediment around
them, may have lain at the bottom of a shallow sea.*

Opportunity *took this panoramic photograph of "Endurance*

to last ninety days. Though *Spirit* had a problem with its software, it had met all its mission goals with all systems fully functioning. *Opportunity* required only minor adjustments and had met all its mission goals as well. With both rovers functioning at top levels, NASA decided to extend the MER mission.

Scientists wanted to learn more about the history of water on Mars. More could be learned from aboveground rock formations. Both *Spirit* and *Opportunity* had photographed interesting rock formations on distant horizons. The rovers' extended mission assignments were to head for these formations for further study.

The rovers continued to explore Mars until September 2004. *Spirit* traveled to a spot named "Columbia Hills." The site was one of seven that scientists hoped *Spirit* might explore on its extended mission. *Opportunity*'s assignment was to explore a crater named "Endurance."

rater" in July 2004 before exploring the crater itself.

The Mars rover mission confirmed that Mars had standing water in its history. This discovery encouraged NASA scientists to expand their plans to explore the planet. The next big question to answer is the one about life on Mars. In a March 23, 2004, press release, Ed Weiler, NASA's associate administrator for space science, talked about further missions for "exploring Mars to learn whether microbes have ever lived there and, ultimately, whether we can."

Glossary

abrasion: Wearing or grinding away by friction.

array: A large number of things.

descent: To go down or lower.

environment: All the things (such as air, soil, and water) that influence life in a given area.

fairing: A smooth covering that reduces drag (wind resistance) on vehicles.

geologist: A person or machine that studies rocks.

jettison: To throw away to lighten the load.

module: An independently operated unit of a spacecraft.

molten: Melted by heat.

panoramic: A wide or complete view of an area.

sediment: Rocks, sand, or dirt carried to a place by water, wind, or a glacier.

spectrometer: An instrument used to measure light waves. Chemical elements radiate energy in the form of light waves. Elements can be identified through light emission (radiation).

stratum, strata (plural): A layer of sediment.

thermal: Having to do with heat or holding in heat.

timetable: A schedule.

For Further Exploration

Books

Kenneth C. Davis, *I Don't Know Much About the Solar System*. New York: HarperCollins, 2001. Fact-filled tour of the solar system in question and answer format.

Don Nardo, *Space Travel*. San Diego: KidHaven, 2003. This colorfully illustrated book describes humanity's travels into space in search of life on other planets. The book includes information about past, present, and future space exploration.

Sally Ride and Tam O'Shaughnessy, *The Mystery of Mars*. New York: Crown, 1999. An exploration of the red planet, the book compares Earth to Mars. It also contains information about early Mars exploration and the possibility of life on the planet.

Web Sites

EdSpace (http://edspace.nasa.gov/index.html). Join NASA's Earth Crew. This multimedia site looks and operates like a video game. Click on pictures to find information, photographs, and more video surprises. Click on a "Knowtron" to get "trivia" on space flights, astronauts, space exploration history, and NASA programs. Fun, fact-filled site.

Mars for Kids (www.nasa.gov). NASA's Mars for Kids site combines animated graphics, photographs, and information about the Mars exploration program. Includes games, activities, and information about special events at NASA.

MarsQuest Online (www.marsquestonline.org/mer). Site sponsors include NASA Jet Propulsion Laboratory, National Science Foundation, Space Science Institute, Digital Library for Earth System Education, and others. Provides kid-level fun facts and lots of pictures from the Mars rovers.

Index

Picture Credits

Lucile Davis loves to do research and share what she has learned with others. She has a wide range of interests including history, the arts, archaeology, geology, and space travel. Her published books include biographies, histories, social studies, and medicine. Ms. Davis lives in Texas.

Babysitting